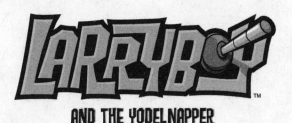

AND THE YODELNAPPER

ZONDERKIDZ

Larryboy and the Yodelnapper
Copyright © 2003 Big Idea, Inc. VEGGIETALES®, character names, likenesses and other indicia are
trademarks of Big Idea, Inc. All rights reserved.

Requests for information should be addressed to:

Zonderkidz, *Grand Rapids, Michigan 49530*

ISBN 978-0-310-70562-8

Written by: Kent Redeker
Editors: Cindy Kenney, Gwen Ellis
Cover and Interior Illustrations: Michael Moore
Cover Design and Art Direction: Paul Conrad, Karen Poth
Interior Design: Holli Leegwater, John Trent, and Karen Poth

Printed in the United States of America

11 12 13 14 15 16 17 18 19 20 /DCI/ 25 24 23 22 21 20 19 18 17 16 15 14 13 12 10 9 8 7 6

VeggieTales

LARRYBOY™

AND THE YODELNAPPER

WRITTEN BY
KENT REDEKER

ILLUSTRATED BY
MICHAEL MOORE

BASED ON THE HIT VIDEO SERIES: LARRYBOY
CREATED BY PHIL VISCHER
SERIES ADAPTED BY TOM BANCROFT

ZONDER**kidz**

ZONDERVAN.com/
AUTHORTRACKER
follow your favorite authors

TABLE OF CONTENTS

CHAPTER 1

HULA HEIDI HAZARD

Mayor Fleming was not at work.
She had taken the day off. She was
skipping merrily through a field of tulips
while gleefully warbling a made-up tune about
marmalade and beach balls.

Why would the mayor of Bumblyburg act in
such a footloose and fancy-free way? Because it was
a splendidly gorgeous day in Bumblyburg! It was the
kind of day where you could almost smell the happiness and carefree-icity in the air—the kind of day
where you wonder why anyone would ever stay
indoors doing algebra problems.

Good citizens all over Bumblyburg were enjoying
the fine morning. Herbert and Wally were grilling
cheese-filled hot dogs. Junior Asparagus was
waterskiing. Even Police Chief Croswell had

decided to enjoy the day by hang gliding off Mount Bumbly while eating a very large snow cone.

But what was Larry the Cucumber doing on this fine, happy, happy spring day? Larry and his faithful butler, Archie, were doing something decidedly unhappy and unspringlike. They were waiting in line.

More specifically, they were standing in line outside of Mr. Snappy's Extremely Gigantic Toy Emporium (which is an unnecessarily long way of saying Mr. Snappy's Great-Big Toy Store).

Why would Larry, or anyone else for that matter, be standing in line on such a fine day? The answer is simple: Hula Heidi.

"I can't wait to get my very own Hula Heidi doll!" said Larry. Hula Heidi was the latest in the Hula Friends line of dolls. Each doll played Hawaiian music and danced its own version of the hula. Since it was the first day anyone could buy Hula Heidi, dozens of Hula Friends lovers were waiting outside the toy store so that they could be among the first to buy one.

"But Master Larry," said Archie. "It's such a beautiful warbling sort of morning! Wouldn't you rather be out skipping through the fields?"

"Archie! I'm surprised at you!" said Larry. "You know how much I want a new Hula Friend. They do the hula...like this!" He began humming Hawaiian music and dancing his own little hula. **"ALOAH-AH-OOOY! AL-WAA-LEE-LOO!"** Unfortunately, Larry's attempt at dancing looked more like a worm trying to put on a leotard than an actual hula dance.

"Yes, yes," said Archie. "I know. But don't you think you might already have *enough* Hula Friends?"

Larry looked shocked. "You don't understand, Archie," answered Larry. "I may have Hula Hillary and Hula Howie and Hula Hannah and Hula Hattie and Hula Harley and Hula Heather and Hula Harry and Hula Henrietta and Hula Hector and Hula Holly and Hula Harriet and Hula Hortence and Hula Hank and Hula Hallie and...and some others, I think, but I don't have Hula *Heidi*. And if I don't have Hula Heidi, I won't have them all, and I *have* to have them *all*!"

CHAPTER 2

STAMPEDE!

At that moment, Archie was just about to tell Larry that he did *not* need them all. In fact Archie was about to say that Larry was spending way too much time playing with his Hula Friends. Archie knew that God doesn't want us to center our lives on material things. He thought Larry should spend more time with his family and his friends. He was even about to say that perhaps it wasn't healthy for someone like Larry to play for days in the basement talking to dolls while wearing a grass skirt and drinking coconut milk.

These are things that Archie wanted to say. But all he ever got the chance to say was **"OOOF,"** for at that moment, the doors of Mr. Snappy's Extremely Gigantic Toy Emporium opened. All of the Hula Friends lovers who had been standing in line pushed and shoved and stomped and stampeded right past Archie, knocking him flat on his stalk!

It was total madness as the most frenzied toy buyers in all of Bumblyburg rushed into the store. Each one of them wanted to be the first to buy a Hula Heidi. They pushed and they shoved. It was the worst pushing and shoving ever seen in Bumblyburg!

Larry found himself near the back of the line. To get closer to the front, he grabbed a pogo stick and attempted to bounce forward. He called, **"I'M COMING, HULA HEIDI!"**

Larry was so excited that he didn't even notice that one of his pogo-bounces knocked a Young Scientist Chemistry Set to the floor. All of the bottles of chemicals broke open, and the contents became mixed together. The mess trickled across the floor, where it oozed into an exhibit—*The World's Biggest Lump of Crazy Clay*. When the chemicals reached the huge lump of Crazy Clay, a strange and unexpected thing began to happen. It was the kind of thing that you never would have guessed: the chemicals caused a reaction that turned The World's Biggest Lump of Crazy Clay into The World's Biggest Lump of Crazy Clay That Could Move Around Like A Giant Amoeba And Liked To Smash Things!

CHAPTER 3

CRAZY CLAY GONE CRAZY

The World's Biggest Lump of Crazy Clay rose up and smashed a whole shelf full of tricycles. The noise was so loud that even the stampeding Hula Heidi lovers stopped to look.

"**AAAAAAUGH!**" said one of the stampeders. "The World's Biggest Lump of Crazy Clay has gone...**CRAZY!**"

Instead of customers rushing to buy toys, customers were now rushing to get away from the giant blue lump of Crazy Clay. It was bad. It was the worst catastrophe that had ever happened at a toy store in Bumblyburg.

"We need a hero of some sort!" shouted Mr. Snappy, the toy-store owner.

Larry realized that this was a job for Bumblyburg's favorite cucumber crime crusader!

He dove under a pile of stuffed animals—but not to hide like a frightened little baby chick. No siree! Moments later he burst forth from the pile as...*Larryboy!*

"I...AM...THAT...HERO!" shouted Larryboy.

Meanwhile, The World's Biggest Lump of Crazy Clay continued to smash its way through the store. Since they were in a toy store, toys were the things that were getting smashed the most. The Crazy Clay picked up a dollhouse and prepared to throw it to the ground.

Larryboy hopped in front of the Crazy Clay. He wasn't about to sit by and let an innocent dollhouse get smashed needlessly.

"Halt, World's Biggest Lump of Crazy Clay!" he shouted. "I don't know why you are so angry with these toys, but I'm sure we can talk about whatever it is that's making you so mad."

The dollhouse came crashing down on Larryboy's head. Apparently the Crazy Clay was in no mood to talk.

"That does it!" said a slightly woozy Larryboy. "Taste my plungers, blob creature!"

Larryboy fired his miraculous plunger ears at The World's Biggest Lump of Crazy Clay. But instead of defeating the creature, the plungers went right through it. The Crazy Clay made a horrible gurgling noise.

That's when Larryboy realized two things: his plungers were of no use in fighting this blob, and he had just made the Crazy Clay really, *really* angry.

"UH-OH," he said as he retracted his plunger ears, now covered in blue Crazy Clay glop.

The World's Biggest Lump of Crazy Clay lunged at him. Larryboy had to think quickly (which is not exactly his specialty). He grabbed a tennis racquet from a shelf and shouted, **"STAY BACK!"** while waving it at the blue blob.

The World's Biggest Lump of Crazy Clay simply seized the racquet and absorbed it into his blue Crazy Clay body.

Next, Larryboy grabbed a paddleball and tried to intimidate the blob with the **BAPPITY-BAPPITY-BAPPITY** sound of the bouncing ball. But the blob snatched the paddleball and absorbed that too.

Larryboy looked around and grabbed a Miss Pretty Pretty doll. He held the doll out and said (in a doll's voice), "Hi! I'm Miss Pretty Pretty. I am so cute. La la la la la! Please don't smash me all to bits, Mr. Blue Crazy Clay Monster! La la la la la!"

Unimpressed, The World's Biggest Lump of Crazy Clay absorbed Miss Pretty Pretty too. (It seemed the cute little dolly routine didn't work on crazed monsters.) Then the Crazy Clay grabbed Larryboy and picked him up off the ground. It looked like Larryboy would be next!

"Hey," said Larryboy. "I've got an idea. How about you and I play a game of badminton? Doesn't that sound like fun?"

Apparently it did not sound like fun to the Crazy Clay.

What apparently *did* sound like fun to the Crazy Clay was to pick up Larryboy and throw *him* to the ground, and that's what it did. Larryboy looked around desperately, grabbing the only thing he could reach…a toy saxophone.

"A toy saxophone?" he shrieked as the Crazy Clay picked him up again. "Why don't they design toys with monster-destroying capabilities?"

Larryboy would have preferred to develop a new plan of attack at that point. However, he was about to be absorbed by The World's Biggest Lump of Crazy Clay, so he did the only thing he could think of. He closed his eyes, blew a long soulful note on the saxophone, and waited to be absorbed.

CHAPTER 4

CLAYMOTION

To Larryboy's great surprise, when he opened his eyes, he had not been absorbed. In fact, The World's Biggest Lump of Crazy Clay set him down and began rocking back and forth to the music.

"Hey! I wasn't absorbed!" said Larryboy. He was so surprised that he stopped saxophoning.

Then the blob stopped swaying and smashed a model train.

"Larryboy!" shouted Archie, who had just made his way into the store. "The Crazy Clay blob seems to *like* the saxophone! Keep playing!"

"What should I play?" asked Larryboy as the blob moved toward him in a way that indicated that more smashing was about to occur.

"Anything!" shouted Archie. "Play anything!"

So Larryboy played the first thing that came into his head, which happened to be "The Song of the Cebu." Once again the Crazy Clay stopped smashing stuff and started swaying to the music. The World's Biggest Lump of Crazy Clay was...*dancing!* It danced the twist, the hustle, and the mashed potato. That Crazy Clay could really rock and roll!

After a few moments of dancing, Larryboy got a great idea. He started playing a lullaby, and before long The World's Biggest Lump of Crazy Clay was sound asleep.

Soon after that, the zookeeper from the Bumblyburg City Zoo arrived to take the sleeping Crazy Clay away.

"AWWW," said Larryboy, looking at the dozing Crazy Clay. "That horrible monster almost killed me, but the Crazy Clay looks so cute when it's sleeping. It was probably just cranky because it needed a nap."

"Well, don't worry, Larryboy," said the zookeeper. "We'll give it a nice home...in a glass cage where it can't ooze through the bars and escape."

"That's a good idea," said Larryboy.

As the zookeeper drove away, Archie hopped up beside Larryboy. "My, my," he said. "That was quite a lot of excitement for a day that started out with standing in line for Hula Heidi."

"Hula Heidi!" exclaimed Larryboy. "I almost forgot!"

Larryboy dove under the pile of stuffed animals again, changed out of his Larryboy costume, and raced to the Hula Friends section.

When he got there, he heard some horrible news.

"Sorry," said Mr. Snappy. "All of the Hula Heidis are gone."

"Oh no!" said Larry. "How can this be?"

"Someone came in and bought up every last Hula Heidi doll," said Mr. Snappy. "Maybe you'd like a slightly smashed model train instead…at a discount?"

"OH, HULA HEIDI!" cried Larry. **"WHY? WHY? WHY??** Why did you let someone buy every last one of you?"

CHAPTER 5

PUDDLE, PUDDLE, MUDDY TROUBLE

Larry went home feeling quite disappointed and turned on all of his lawn sprinklers so he would have mud puddles to jump in. He always jumped in mud puddles when he was upset. Today, Larryboy was *very* upset…and *ve-e-ery* muddy. Archie chased Larry around with a towel, trying to wipe him clean. But Larry just splashed Archie with mud too. If Archie didn't cheer up Larry soon, neither one of them would be clean enough to go into the house!

"But Master Larry! Think of all the Hula Friends you already have!" said Archie looking at all of Larry's Hula Friends he had been pulling along in a little red wagon. The Hula Friends were dancing cheerfully to the rhythm of the islands. Larry looked at them, but it didn't cheer him up.

"Look at Hula Hank!" said Archie. "See his cute little ukulele. Isn't he cutesy-wootsy?"

"Take them away! They're mocking me! I know what they're thinking behind their pleasant Hawaiian smiles! They're thinking, **YOU DON'T HAVE HULA HEIDI! YOU DON'T HAVE US ALL!** That's what they're *really* thinking! They're

thinking it so loud, I can even hear them! I'm incomplete! In-com-plete!"

Archie was beginning to worry about Larry. He knew it wouldn't really make Larry happy even if he could get the latest Hula Friend. But obviously, Larry had not learned that lesson yet. So Archie decided that maybe the best thing to do would be to get his friend's mind off of Hula Heidi.

"Well, Master Larry, you can just keep on jumping in mud puddles, but I'm going to go get ready."

"Ready for what?" asked Larry.

"Have you forgotten? Tonight is the first night of the *Bumblyburg Yodeling Festival*! *And*…I recently found out that world-famous yodeler Einger Warblethroat III is performing!"

"Einger Warblethroat III?" shouted Larry. "He is my very favorite yodeler of all time! He's the only one in the world who can yodel and play the accordion at the same time!"

Archie's strategy worked. Larry forgot all about Hula Heidi. He started hopping back to the mansion where he could get ready for the concert. Archie hopped after him. "Larry, don't track mud all over the floor," he called.

CHAPTER 6

EINGER WARBLETHROAT III

Larry, Archie, and everyone
else in Bumblyburg gathered at the
Bumblyburg Music Hall for the opening night
of the *Bumblyburg Yodeling Festival*. Everyone
in Bumblyburg was excited; they *loved* yodeling.
In fact, they loved yodeling even more than they
loved mud wrestling!

Mayor Fleming hopped up onto the stage. "Good
evening friends! Let's give a great big warble welcome
to Einger Warblethroat III!"

The citizens of Bumblyburg cheered loudly as
Einger Warblethroat III made his way onstage with
his accordion. Larry cheered loudest of all.

Einger began yodeling, **"YODEEL-EEIDEY-IDDEY-
EEIDY. YODEEL-EEIDEY-IDDEY-EEIDY. YODEEL-EEI-
DEY-IDDEY-EEIDY-OOO."** (It was a famous

yodeling song about a two-headed yak and his favorite lollipop.)

Then, right in the middle of the yodeling, there was another sound, a sound that didn't sound like yodeling at all. It sounded a lot like someone was tearing a hole in the roof. And, as a matter of fact, that was exactly what was happening.

Larry and everyone else watched as a glass tube extended through the hole in the roof. Down, down it came and **WHOOSH!** It sucked Einger Warblethroat III and his accordion right through the roof with a little **PFFFT** sound.

Everyone applauded wildly.

"Yea!" shouted Larry. "That Einger Warblethroat III sure knows how to put on a great show!"

Mayor Fleming dashed onstage and yelled, "Walloping

Warblethroat! Citizens of Bumblyburg, that was not part of the show! Einger Warblethroat III has been…*yodelnapped!*"

The audience gasped.

"Is there a hero in the house?" asked Mayor Fleming. Larry realized that once again, **I…AM…THAT…HERO!**

He leaped to his feet and shouted, **"I AM…"**

"Larry!" Archie whispered with a nudge. "Don't give away your secret identity!"

"Oh yeah. I forgot," Larry whispered back.

"Yes, Larry?" said Mayor Fleming. "Did you have something you wanted to say?"

Larry realized that everyone was now looking at him. He tried to think quickly. "I am…I am…um…I am going to go to the bathroom!"

He rushed out the door and headed to the bathroom, "Whew! That was close. But telling them I was on the way to the bathroom was a really smart thing to do."

Archie shrugged nervously. "When you gotta go, you gotta go."

Moments later it was Larryboy who rushed into the music hall. **"I…AM…THAT…HERO!"**

"Larryboy!" said Mayor Fleming. "How warbly wonderful!

We're mighty glad to see you! Einger Warblethroat III has been whisked away!"

"Don't worry, Mayor. Larryboy is on the case!" said Larryboy. "Plungers away!"

He shot his plunger ears up through the hole in the roof and pulled himself upwards. Unfortunately he kinda missed the hole and ended up bonking his head on the ceiling.

"I'm OK!" he said as he dangled from his plunger cords. Again he tried to flip himself up through the hole, but he was a little woozy from hitting his head and only succeeded in smacking his face against the ceiling.

Archie winced. "I'm still OK!" said Larryboy. Finally he managed to pull himself up so that his nose stuck through the hole. Then he used his nose to pull the rest of his body through just in time to see a helicopter flying away. He could see Einger's face pressed against the window.

Larryboy launched a plunger at the helicopter, but it was too far away to reach. Larryboy had no way to chase them. His Larryplane was back at the Larrycave.

As he helplessly watched the helicopter fly away, he faintly heard Einger cry, **"HEEEELLLP-EE-HEEDY-HOODDY-OOODY HEELLLP-EE-OOODY-OO!"**

CHAPTER 7

GREEDY GRETA AND THE PUDDING GLOP

Later that night, Einger Warblethroat III
found himself inside a glass tube in a room in a
deep, deep, sub-, sub-basement of a large castle.
He looked around and said, "Would you look at
that!" All of the rest of the world's greatest yodelers
were there too, and they were also trapped inside
glass tubes.

About now you may be thinking, *Who could be so
rotten and villainous as to yodelnap all of the world's
greatest yodelers and deprive the citizens of
Bumblyburg, as well as the rest of the world, of
quality yodeling entertainment? Who would be so
greedy as to only think of his or her own yodeling needs?*

Well, as it so happened, Einger
Warblethroat III had those very same
questions on

his mind. "Who would ever do such a confounded crazy thing?" he cried.

Suddenly, an easy chair in the center of the room swung around toward him. In it sat a green zucchini wearing a jewel-encrusted tiara and a pearl necklace. "I would," she said.

"And just who might *you* be?" asked Einger.

"I am Greedy Greta, the greedy zucchini," she said.

Greedy Greta lived in a castle in a mountainous alpine village just outside Bumblyburg. Her uncle Green Gregor, the gruesome zucchini, had given her the castle. Green Gregor had made his fortune selling rare bottle caps. He had collected them when he was just a wee zucchini and had passed all of his great wealth to Greedy Greta as an inheritance. Now Greedy Greta had more money than she knew how to spend. But did her money make her happy? It did not!

So Greta decided maybe she would be happy if she bought whatever she wanted. This, however, didn't make her happy either. Then she realized that there were some things that even she didn't have enough money to buy. So she began to steal things. But that didn't make her happy

either. Still she kept trying. She was convinced that if she just had a few more things, she would finally attain true happiness.

But why would she yodelnap all of the world's greatest yodelers? Einger Warblethroat III had that very same question, so he asked, "Why would you yodelnap all of the world's greatest yodelers?"

"I *love* yodeling!" said Greedy Greta.

"Yeah, but so does everyone else!" said Einger.

Greedy Greta got up from her easy chair at the center of the room and made her way over to Einger. "I listened

to yodeling concerts and I listened to the CDs, but that wasn't enough for me! I wanted *more* yodeling! So I decided I would kidnap a yodeler so that I could make him yodel whenever I wanted."

"That's pretty greedy," said Einger.

"But then I realized that I wasn't happy with just one yodeler. If I was going to be happy, I would have to yodelnap **ALL** of the world's greatest yodelers for myself. That way I could have them at my beck and call for my own private yodeling concert whenever I wished!"

"But there's one thing you didn't think about," said

Einger. "I won't yodel for you! I *never* perform for yodel-nappers!"

"Oh, I think you will!" said Greedy Greta as she sat back down in her easy chair. "If you don't, I will press this button right here."

"I won't," insisted Einger.

So Greta pressed the button on the side of her chair, and a glop of smelt-flavored pudding fell onto Einger's head.

"EEEEWW!" said Einger. "Smelt-flavored pudding!"

"Our family recipe!" beamed Greta.

CHAPTER 8

MOPPING THINGS UP

The next day, Larry rode the elevator up to the offices of the *Daily Bumble* newspaper where he worked as a janitor. He didn't really enjoy working as a janitor. He didn't need the money. He already had a mansion and a butler. Besides, being a janitor involved *way* too much mopping, at least that's what Larry thought.

He only took the job at the *Daily Bumble,* so he could eavesdrop on the reporters. Then he'd be the first to know when there was trouble that needed to be handled by Larryboy.

As the elevator climbed to the top floor, Larry's mop rang.

That's right, his mop rang.

Archie had installed a hi-tech feature in

Larry's mop so that he and Larry could talk with each other whenever they needed to.

Everyone in the elevator looked at the funny janitor with the ringing mop. Larry threw the wet end of the mop over his head. This wasn't just to avoid the funny looks he was getting. Throwing the mop over his head was the way he activated the video screen that let him communicate with Archie.

"How are you doing, Master Larry?" asked Archie, as the image of his face appeared on the mop video screen.

"I'm on the elevator, just about to report for work,"

replied Larry.

"What? But, Larry, you left for work more than an hour ago!"

"I know, but I stopped for a jelly doughnut," said Larry.

Archie sighed. "Oh well," he said. "Listen, Larry, we need to find out as much information as we can about the yodelnapper. So if any of the reporters at the *Daily Bumble* have any news, hold your mop up to his or her mouth."

"EEEEW! Why would I want to do that?" asked Larry.

"Because the microphone in your mop will transmit the information to me, and then we can analyze the data in the Larrycomputer," said Archie.

"OK, over and out!" said Larry as the doors of the elevator opened. Larry tried to hop out of the elevator, but the mop was still draped over his head and he tripped. Before Larry could get up, the elevator doors closed on his head.

"OWWWWIEEEE!" yelled Larry.

"Are you OK?" asked a voice nearby.

Larry pulled the mop off of his head and looked up to see Vicki Cucumber, the photographer for the *Daily Bumble*, looking down at him. *Oh no!* thought Larry. *Why does Vicki, the most beautiful cucumber in all of Bumblyburg, always show up when I'm in the most embarrassing positions?*

"Oh, yeah, I'm fine." he said nervously.

"Then why are you lying on the floor, letting the elevator doors close on your head?" Vicki asked.

"Well, you see, as a janitor, I have to look for dirt from every angle! Dirt can be sneaky! And grime! Grime is good at hiding in the elevator doors. Sometimes I have to get down and look real close!"

"Well, Larry, that's really...fascinating. But I have to

run. We're having a big meeting about the yodelnapper story. Bye!" She hopped away quickly.

Larry felt really silly, and he wanted to run away and hide. But he knew that he had to see what information he could get about the yodelnapper, so he—hopped over to where the staff was talking.

"I want all available reporters to see what they can find out about the yodelnapping." said Bob. "This is the biggest story in Bumblyburg since the mayor accidentally glued his moustache to the garbage truck!"

"I hear this yodelnapping goes deeper than just the *Bumblyburg Yodeling Festival*," said Vicki.

"Yeah," chimed in rookie reporter Junior Asparagus. "Yodelers are disappearing from all over the world!"

Larry stuck his mop right in Junior's face. "Um...could you repeat that?"

"Yodelers are disappearing from all over the world," said Junior, trying to brush the stray mop strands out of his nose.

"OH NO!" said Larry. "Who could be doing such dastardly deeds?"

"No one knows," said Vicki. Larryboy quickly shoved

the mop in her face. "All the usual supervillains like Awful Alvin, the Alchemist, and the Emperor and Lampy are already behind bars."

"Looks like we've got a new supervillain out there," said Junior.

"A dastardly new yodelnapping supervillian on the loose!" said Bob. "Hey…that sounds like a good headline! Larry! What are you doing?" he asked as Larry jabbed the mop in front of Bob's face.

"Oh, um, I…uh…I thought I saw some grime on your face, and I thought I should mop it up," Larry explained as he wiped Bob's face with the mop.

"Larry!" growled Bob with a scowl.

"Sorry." Larry quickly moved the mop a little farther away.

"Don't ever mop me up again, unless I specifically ask you to!" snapped Bob, hopping away angrily. But moments later he returned. "Well, what are all of you waiting for?" he shouted to his reporters. "This story isn't going to report itself!"

The news staff scattered, eager to get the big story. And Larry was left standing alone with his mop.

Just then the mop rang, so Larry threw it over his head.

"Did you get all of that?" Larry asked the video image of Archie.

"Yes, but I'm afraid this case is worse than we thought! We don't even know who the yodelnapper is!" exclaimed Archie.

"What are we going to do?" asked Larry.

"I don't know," said Archie. "Maybe you should ask Bok Choy's advice when you get to superhero class tonight."

CHAPTER 9

SOB CHOY

Bok Choy stood at the front of the class, crying like a big baby chicken that just lost his favorite pair of red rubber galoshes.

Larryboy and the other superheroes had never seen their teacher like that before. Quite frankly they were worried about him.

"I can't believe he's gone!" sobbed Bok Choy. "Why would someone yodelnap Einger Warblethroat III? Why, why, why?"

Einger Warblethroat III was Bok Choy's favorite yodeler. He liked to listen to Einger's CDs every morning as he did his superhero exercises.

But now Einger was gone and Bok Choy was taking it really hard.

"Are you OK, sir?" asked Electro Melon.

Bok Choy tried to compose himself. "Yes," he said. "Yes, please forgive me. I'm going through a tough time. But as an ex-superhero, I must remember that I've faced tougher challenges than this." He took a deep breath before continuing. "So, let's get to tonight's lesson, shall we? Tonight, I want to tell you heroes about the dangers of materialism."

Larryboy leaned over to Dark Crow, a grape who wished he wasn't vegetable. If anyone could judge Bok

Choy's disposition, it was him. "You think he's going to be all right?" Larryboy asked.

"I don't know," said Dark Crow. "Warblethroat was Master Choy's favorite."

"I hope he's OK. I was gonna ask him for some advice after class."

"I'm OK now," continued Bok Choy, blowing his nose. "Okeydokey. A hero should not base his happiness on material things," said Bok Choy. "Can anyone give me an example of a material thing?"

"Money!" said Lemon Twister.

"A fancy utility belt," Scarlet Tomato chimed in.

"A supersonic stealth plane," added Dark Crow.

"Good! Good! Any more?"

"The complete works of Enger Warblethroat III on CD?" asked Larryboy.

Bok Choy broke down sobbing again. "Oh, my poor Einger! My poor, poor Einger! Come back! Come back, Einger!"

"What?" asked Larryboy as everyone turned to look at him.

"Um…sir, would you like to take a break for a few minutes?" asked Lemon Twister.

"No," said Bok Choy. "I will finish the lesson. Ahem. If all you want in life is more material things, you will never feel like you have enough. You will never be satisfied. You will always want more and more, and this will make you miserable! To find lasting happiness, it is better to focus on the important things, like thinking more about others than you do about yourself. That's what will bring you lasting happiness."

Bok Choy took a moment to blow his nose.

"Turn in your superhero handbooks to section 21, paragraph 5, subsection 10. 'Whoever loves money never has money enough; whoever loves wealth is never satisfied with his income.' Think well upon this lesson. Are there any questions?"

"Yeah," said Larryboy. "I have a question about the supervillain who yodelnapped Einger Warblethroat the Thi…"

Bok Choy let out a wail of despair. "Einger! Einger! Einger! I want my Warblethroat!" He began beating his head against his desk.

"Um…never mind," said Larryboy.

CHAPTER 10

LEDERHOSEN!

That evening Larryboy went back to the Larrycave.

"So, did Bok Choy have any good ideas on how to catch the yodelnapper?" asked Archie.

"Well...no."

"I see," said Archie. "Oh well, no matter. I came up with a splendid plan all by myself!"

"That's great!" said Larryboy excitedly. "What is it? Tell me, tell me! What's the plan? Tell me the plan!"

Minutes later Larryboy hopped out from the Larryboy special-disguises changing room. Only he didn't look so much like Larryboy anymore. He was now wearing lederhosen and a wooden shoe over his Larryboy costume. A fake mustache and fake glasses worn over his mask complemented the lederhosen. In addition, he was pulling a life-sized toy sheep alongside himself.

"This is the plan?" asked a confused and embarrassed Larryboy.

"Well, yes," explained Archie. "It's *part* of the plan. See, you're going to pose as a famous yodeler named Noodle Blabberbop."

"Ooh! I like the name! Blabberbop. It's fun to say. Blabberbop! Blabberbop! Blabberbop!" said Larryboy.

"Then, as Noodle Blabberbop, you will perform at the *Bumblyburg Music Festival.*"

"But what if the yodelnapper shows up?" asked Larryboy.

"Then you'll be yodelnapped!"

"But Archie, I don't *want* to be yodelnapped!" said Larryboy.

"Don't worry, Larryboy," said Archie. "It's all part of the plan. You're the bait for our trap. You will let the yodelnapper take you to where the other yodelers are being held. Then, you will escape with the help of some wonderful gadgets I've installed in this toy sheep. Once you escape, you can free the yodelers and capture the yodelnapper! Do you understand the plan?"

"Blabberbop! Blabberbop! Blabberbop!" Larryboy exclaimed gleefully.

"OK then. The first thing we have to do is to make sure that the yodelnapper knows about your upcoming performance."

"Did you say 'performance'?" asked Larryboy.

CHAPTER 11

BLABBERBOP BLABS TO THE *BUMBLE*

The next day, "Noodle Blabberbop" (and his toy sheep) held a press conference at the offices of the *Daily Bumble* to announce that he would be performing at the Bumblyburg Music Hall.

Everyone at the *Daily Bumble* was excited by the news. Everyone except Bob, that is. Bob was annoyed that the floors hadn't been mopped because Larry the janitor hadn't shown up for work yet.

"That's right," said Larryb...um...Noodle. "My appearance at the Music Hall will prove to everyone that I am truly the world's best yodeler!"

"If you're the world's best yodeler, how come we've never heard of you?" asked Junior Asparagus.

"Well...um...that's

because I've spent the last seven years in…outer space. Yeah! I've been the yodeling ambassador to Jupiter!"

"OOOOH!" said Junior. "I've always wanted to go to Jupiter! What are the aliens from Jupiter like?"

"Um…no more questions about Jupiter," said Noodle. "I was an ambassador *and* a spy! It was all very, very *top secret*," he added. Larryboy didn't like having to pretend he was someone else. It made him very uncomfortable.

Vicki took a picture of Noodle as the other reporters continued to ask him questions. She leaned toward Junior and whispered, "Does Noodle look familiar to you?"

"No, why?" asked Junior.

"I don't know. There's just something about him. I think he's kinda cute!" said Vicki with that look on her face that she normally only got when Larryboy was around. Junior just rolled his eyes.

"Please take plenty of pictures!" said Noodle. "I want to be on the front page, so that *everyone* will know about my performance!"

"I think we can put you on the front page," said Editor Bob. "Unless there's a bigger story today… like a story about all the horrible things I'm gonna do to our janitor

when he finally shows up!"

Noodle gulped nervously.

"Noodle, one more question," said Junior. "Aren't you afraid of the yodelnapper?"

"Absolutely not!" said Noodle. "Just let that yodelnapper *try* to nab me! I'm not the least little itty-bitty bit afraid!"

CHAPTER 12

GREEDY GRETA GETS GRATUITOUSLY GREEDY

Back at Greedy Greta's castle, Greta sat down in her easy chair with fourteen copies of the *Daily Bumble*.

"Why do you have so many copies?" asked Einger, who was still trapped inside his glass tube.

"I have never been satisfied with just one copy of the paper," said Greedy Greta. "So I follow the paperboy around every morning and take papers from my neighbors' porches. But I always leave each neighbor a quarter for them."

"That sounds frightfully greedy!" said Einger.

"Quiet down and yodel for me while I read my paper, Yodelboy!"

Einger, not wanting smelt-flavored pudding dumped onto his head again, began yodeling vigorously as Greta began reading the *Daily Bumble*.

As she looked at the front page, she couldn't help but see the picture of Noodle Blabberbop.

"What's this?" cried Greedy Greta. "Another yodeler? This means there's a yodeler out there that I don't have! And he says he's the greatest yodeler in the world!"

"But Greta," said Einger. "Don't you think…"

"Who told you to stop yodeling?" she shrieked. She

was so angry about not having *all* of the world's best yodelers that she pressed the button on her chair and dropped smelt-flavored pudding onto the heads of all the yodelers.

"This Noodle Blabberbop says he's not the least little itty-bitty bit afraid of being yodelnapped. Well, we'll just see about that!"

CHAPTER 13

ARCHIE'S PLAN GETS A LITTLE CLOGGED

The next day, Noodle Blabberbop and Archie stood behind the stage curtain of the Bumblyburg Music Hall. "Well, this is it." said Archie. "Your big performance!"

Mayor Fleming appeared onstage. "I'm so excited, I just want to blabber on and on about it! Let me introduce to you Noodle Blabberbop and his toy sheep!"

Everyone applauded as Noodle hopped from behind the stage curtain, wearing his lederhosen and wooden shoe. He hopped toward the front of the stage, pulling his toy sheep. But then, suddenly, he stopped. His eyes opened wide with panic.

Everyone in Bumblyburg was there...and looking right at *him*.

He darted back behind the curtain.

Archie rushed up to him.

"Larrybo…um…I mean Noodle, what's wrong? You have to go back onstage!"

"But…but…everyone's out there. Bob, Junior…*Vicki*! They were all *watching* me!"

"Of course," said Archie. "They came to hear you yodel."

"But Archie, I just remembered something," said Noodle. "I don't know *how* to yodel!"

"You don't have to yodel," said Archie. "The yodelnapper will yodelnap you."

"But what if he doesn't show up?" asked Noodle.

"Don't worry! The yodelnapper *will* show up. Now you get back out there!" said Archie as he shoved Noodle back onstage.

There was another brief moment of applause, followed by complete silence. Noodle looked out at the crowd. They looked back.

No yodelnapper.

"So...um...nice weather we're having, huh?" said Noodle nervously.

The crowd looked back at him. Still no yodelnapper.

"Hey!" said Noodle. "Did you hear the one about the one-eyed pirate and the cantaloupe?"

Someone from the back of the music hall yelled, "Yodel already!"

Noodle knew he couldn't stall any longer. The time had come...to fake it.

"YODEL YODEL YODEL YODEL YODEL YODEL YODEL YODEL YODEL YODEL," sang Noodle.

The crowd began to frown. "He's not even yodeling!" said Bob.

"Yeah, he's just singing the word 'yodel' over and over," said Junior.

The crowd began to boo. Noodle began to sweat. And lederhosen are not very comfortable once you start to sweat in them! *Where is that yodelnapper?*

The booing got louder. *I gotta do something*, Noodle realized.

And so, out of desperation, Noodle did the only thing he could think of doing. He began clog dancing.

CLOPPITY-CLOPPITY went his one wooden shoe.

The crowd stopped booing. In fact they started cheering instead. Apparently the citizens of Bumblyburg loved clog dancing almost as much as they loved yodeling!

As the cheering increased, Noodle began to enjoy him-self. *They love my dancing! They love me! I've clogged my way into their hearts!*

But, just as Noodle was beginning to envision a clog-ging world tour, a glass tube crashed through the ceiling and sucked him and his toy sheep up into an awaiting helicopter.

He had been yodelnapped!

CHAPTER 14

LOTS OF SMELT-FLAVORED PUDDING

Greedy Greta stood Noodle inside the glass tube next to all the other yodelers.

"Finally," said Greedy Greta, "I have *all* of the world's greatest yodelers! Even the great yodel ambassador to Jupiter!"

"So, *you're* the yodelnapper!" exclaimed Noodle.

"That's right! I, Greedy Greta, the Greedy Zucchini, have yodelnapped all of the world's greatest yodelers to satisfy my need to have yodeling upon command!

"That's pretty greedy," said Noodle. "I mean, yodel-napping one yodeler is bad enough, but yodelnapping *all* of us?

"What's the point if you don't have the whole set?" she replied. "Now stop talking and yodel for me!"

"Um... I can't," he said.

"You'd better do it," said Einger from the next tube. "You don't want to make her mad."

"Sorry, but I can't," said Noodle.

"Wrong answer!" said Greedy Greta as she pressed the button and dumped smelt-flavored pudding onto his head.

"EEEECH! I got pudding down my lederhosen!" yelped Noodle.

"Yodel, Noodle! Yodel!" Greta demanded.

"Well, the truth is, I don't know how," said Noodle.

"Wrong answer!" said Greedy Greta as more smelt-flavored pudding fell onto Noodle's head..

"Just give me a second to explain!" said Noodle. "Besides, I really hate having smelt-flavored pudding dumped onto my head."

"I know! Everyone does! Now, are you going to yodel or do you want another dose?" asked Greta.

"I can't yodel because..."

SPLAT. Another glob of smelt-flavored pudding fell onto his head.

"Wait! Let me explain!" begged Noodle.

SPLAT!

"I can do this all day!" said Greedy Greta. "I've got a whole lot of pudding!"

"But I really don't know how to yodel," said Noodle.

"That's absurd! How can you be a world-famous yodeler if you don't know how to yodel?" asked Greedy Greta.

"Because I'm not really a world-famous yodeler," said Noodle. At that moment, he ripped off his Noodle disguise, revealing his true identity. **"I...AM...THAT...HERO!"**

"Larryboy!" exclaimed a shocked Greedy Greta. "I didn't know you could yodel."

"I can't," said Larryboy. "I came to save the yodelers!"

"HOORAY-EEDI-EEIDI-OOODLE-IIEDY-YAY-YAY!" cheered the yodelers.

"I demand that you release me and the yodelers this instant!" said Larryboy.

"No!" said Greedy Greta.

"Oh," said Larryboy.

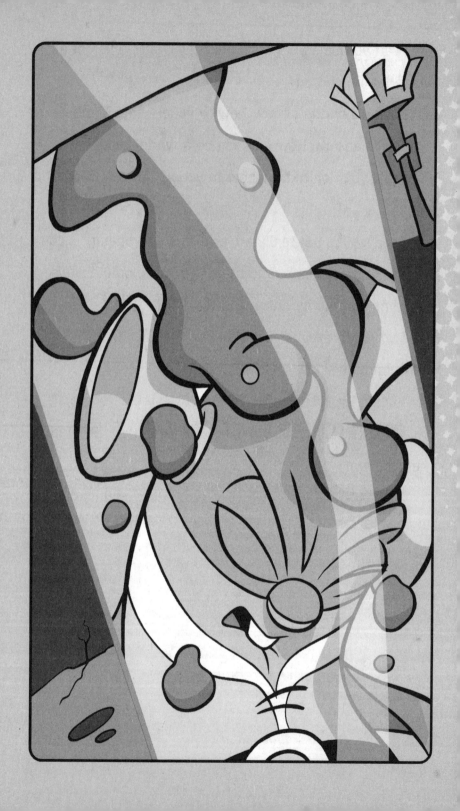

CHAPTER 15

THE HARD WAY

This was disappointing for Larryboy. He had hoped that Greedy Greta would just sorta give up, let everyone go, and turn from her wicked ways. But it looked like he'd have to do things the hard way.

"OK, Greedy Greta, you give me no choice."

"And you give me no choice but to dump even *more* pudding onto your head!"

She dumped more pudding onto his head.

"Now cut that out!"

Then she dumped more pudding onto his head.

"That's really starting to get annoy... "

She dumped even *more* pudding onto his head!

At that point, Larryboy decided that maybe he'd better just shut his big mouth before the whole glass tube, in which he was still trapped, would be filled with smelt-flavored pudding. He also decided that it was time to activate the escape mechanism Archie had installed inside the toy sheep.

Larryboy fired his plunger ears at the sheep. When he retracted them, each ear was plugged with sheep wool. Then he pressed a button on the sheep labeled **PRESS TO ESCAPE.**

The sheep gave out a high-pitched **"BAAAAA!"** causing the glass tube holding Larryboy to break open. Greta quickly hopped out of the way.

Unfortunately for Larryboy, when the tube broke open, all of the pudding inside it carried him along like a smelt-flavored tidal wave. Finally Larryboy came to a stop and stood up, covered in even more smelt-flavored pudding.

"YUCKY!" he said.

Luckily Archie had installed some other special equipment inside the toy sheep. Larryboy pushed another button and a robotic arm holding a squeegee came out of the sheep's back and wiped Larryboy clean.

"Thanks, toy sheep!" said Larryboy.

"BAAAA," said the toy sheep, but Larryboy didn't hear him. He still had wool in his ears.

"Now it's time to free the yodelers!" said Larryboy. He hopped over to a panel labeled **YODELER'S RELEASE.** He pulled a lever and the glass tubes holding the yodelers sank into the floor, and the yodelers were free.

"YAAAY-YAY-YAY-EEIDY-IIEDY-EEIDY-OOO!" cheered the yodelers.

"You'll never get away with this, Larryboy!" cried Greta.

"What?" asked Larryboy. "Hold on a second." He removed the wool that was still sticking out of his ears. "What did you say?"

"I said you'll never get away with this! I won't let you take my yodeler collection. How could I ever be happy without all of the world's best yodelers belonging only to me? If I don't have them all, I'll never be satisfied!"

"You know," said Larryboy, "this reminds me of something my superhero instructor, Bok Choy, said in class the other day: 'Whosoever loves money never has money enough; whoever loves wealth is never satisfied with his income.'"

"What's that supposed to mean?" sneered Greedy Greta.

"It means that if all you want in life is to gain material

things like money or supersonic jets or really cool plungers or…"

"Or all of the world's best yodelers," added Einger.

"Right! If you base your happiness on material things, you'll never feel like you have enough. You'll never be satisfied, and that will make you miserable," said Larryboy.

"If you think your little speech is going to get me to give up my collection, then I think you're wearing your plungers too tight!" said Greedy Greta.

As she said this, she flipped a switch that opened a trapdoor in the floor underneath Larryboy and the other yodelers.

"AAAAAAAUGH!" said Larryboy as he and the yodelers fell into a dark room.

"Just a minute," said Larryboy. "I have a flashlight in here somewhere."

Larryboy began pulling gadgets from his utility belt. He found a saw, an electric fan, a feather duster, a back scratcher, a mousetrap, but no flashlight.

"Hey," said Einger Warblethroat. "Do you hear something?"

Larryboy and the yodelers all listened in the darkness surrounding them. They *could* hear something. It seemed to be coming from the shadows.

Was it the sound of marching feet and…Hawaiian music?

CHAPTER 16

LARRYBOY COMPLETES HIS COLLECTION

Frightened, Larryboy and the yodelers stood close together. Finally Larryboy dug a little deeper and found his flashlight. He shined it around the dark room. In the light, they could see hundreds of dolls marching toward them.

"Oh boy! Hula Friends!" said Larryboy.

Greedy Greta looked down at them through the trapdoor.

"Meet *my* Hula Friends," she cackled.

"You like Hula Friends?" asked Larryboy.

"I'm a big fan of the Hula Friends! I even bought every last Hula Heidi at Mr. Snappy's Extremely Gigantic Toy Emporium."

"That was *you*?" asked Larryboy.

"That's right!" said Greta. "I can't get

enough Hula Friends! I buy as many as I can get, but I always want more and more! I've got quite a collection! But unfortunately for you, I've modified these Hula Friends to *attack*! You'll never escape from them! Attack! Attack, my hula minions!"

"What are we gonna DOO-IEEDEE-OOH-OODY-OOODY-IIEDY-OOH?" asked Einger.

"Well, I know what I'm going to do!" said Larryboy. "If Greedy Greta doesn't want those dolls any more, I'm gonna complete my Hula Friends collection!"

Larryboy shot out one of his plunger ears and snagged a Hula Heidi.

"Hula Heidi! At last, you are mine!" he said as the other Hula Friends continued to advance.

"But…but what about them?" asked Einger.

Larryboy turned and looked at the other Hula Friends. "You're right," he said. "Why have just one Hula Heidi when I could have one hundred!"

Larryboy rushed toward the other Hula Friends, but the yodelers jumped on top of him and held him down.

"What are you doing?" asked Larryboy. "All of the Hula Friends can be mine! I need more Hula Friends!"

"But Larryboy," said Einger, "don't you remember what your teacher said? If you base your happiness on getting more and more material things, you'll never feel like you have enough and you'll be miserable. If you can't think of anything but Hula Friends, you'll become just like Greedy Greta, the Greedy Zucchini!"

Larryboy thought about this for a moment and realized that what Einger said was true.

"You're right," said Larryboy. "I can't let myself become like her. She's a villain, and I...AM...THAT...HERO! I'm supposed to stop her!"

"Great," said Einger. "There's just one problem."

"What's that?" asked Larryboy.

Einger pointed to the ever-advancing Hula Friends who were practically upon them. "We're about to get hula-ed!"

The Hula Friends were getting ready to leap on top of Larryboy and the yodelers. "Stay back!" said Larryboy. "I'll handle this!"

Larryboy fought valiantly. He fired his plungers into the oncoming Hula swarm time and time again. But there were just too many of them. For every Hula doll he knocked down, there were dozens more to attack him with their ukuleles, their leis, and their enchanting island rhythms.

Soon they had wrestled him to the ground and were taking turns dancing on his head. "Hey! That hurts, you know!" said Larryboy. But the Hula Friends did not listen to Larryboy's cries for mercy. Greedy Greta had changed them from cute island dancers to vicious island meanies. Larryboy knew he had to retreat and come up with a new plan. He fired one of his plungers straight up, where it stuck to the ceiling. He then pulled himself up, shaking loose the Hula Friends that were still clinging to him. Finally he was free of the Hula Friends.

"Ha!" shouted Greedy Greta. "The yodelers are no match for my hula army!"

"There are too many of them!" Larryboy shouted to the yodelers.

"This looks like the end for us," sighed Einger as he played a sad little tune on his accordion.

"Einger! Your accordion!" Larryboy shouted down to Einger. "I just got a great idea! Do you know any polka music?"

"Sure," said Einger.

"Play a polka!" said Larryboy. "The Hula Friends may be Hawaiian, but no one can resist the crazy syncopation of a polka!"

Einger began playing a lively polka as the Hula Friends marched toward them.

Larryboy dropped back to the ground in front of the Hula dolls and began singing a song his Grampy Cucumber taught him years before: "The Purple Pickle Polka."

GO TO THE STORE AND BRUSH YOUR TEETH,
JUMP IN THE POOL WITH A CHRISTMAS WREATH,
AND THAT'S THE WAY WE DO, THE PURPLE PICKLE POLKA!

DRINK SOME SOAP AND FLY A KITE,
HOLD YOUR BREATH WITH ALL YOUR MIGHT,
AND THAT'S THE WAY WE DO, THE PURPLE PICKLE POLKA!

JUMP ON THE CHAIR WITH SHINY SHOES,
GO TO THE BEACH AND LOOK FOR CLUES.
BLINK YOUR EYES, CUSTARD PIES, PASTURIZE, DRAGON FLIES,
AND THAT'S THE WAY WE DO THE PURPLE PICKLE POLKA!
HEY! THAT'S THE WAY WE DO THE PURPLE PICKLE POLKA!

As Larryboy sang, the Hula Friends became confused. They were made to hula...but they couldn't resist the polka madness! They began to hop-step-close-step in time with the music.

But their little joints weren't made for such lively dancing. Soon their arms and legs began to spark, then they began to give off smoke. They short-circuited and fell over, broken.

"What have you done?" cried Greedy Greta. "You've destroyed all of my beautiful Hula Friends!"

"I guess I just learned a lesson," replied Larryboy. "Hula Friends are fun, and they're fun to play with. But

God wants us to remember that there are other, more important things than collecting material goods. And for me, one of those things is protecting Bumblyburg from villains like you!"

Larryboy launched one of his plunger ears up through the trapdoor and pulled himself up to the room where Greedy Greta was standing.

"YIKES," said Greedy Greta. She fled into an elevator, and the doors closed behind her. Larryboy watched as the lights on the elevator showed that Greta was going all the way to the top of the castle.

"Guess, I'll have to take the stairs," said Larryboy.

CHAPTER 17

THE SHEEP THAT BROKE THE HELICOPTER'S BACK

A few minutes later, Greedy Greta was on the castle's helicopter launching pad at the top of the castle, getting ready to escape. "Larryboy may have defeated my attack Hula Friends, but he'll never catch *me*! But if I have to escape, I'm going to take my things with me!" she cried.

Greta was loading everything she could into her helicopter. She had already loaded her bed, her bathtub, a set of potholders that looked like kittens, a toilet brush, a half-eaten doughnut, a ceramic statue of a poodle eating a marshmallow, all her lobster bibs, a giant swirly lollipop, a solar-powered waffle iron, twenty-four cases of gum, her blue fuzzy-bunny blanket, her salmon-flavored pillows, a jump

rope, seventy-six trombones, finger paints, her refrigerator magnet collection, the TV antenna, X-ray goggles, a broken hockey stick, a moldy lump of cheese, a throne, a partridge in a pear tree, and...well, just about everything else she owned too.

She just couldn't bear to leave anything behind.

"There," she said at last. "That's everything! I can keep all of my wonderful, wonderful stuff—and still escape!"

Just then Larryboy opened the stairway door and hopped outside, pulling the toy sheep behind him.

Exhausted from rushing up the stairs, he panted, "Who knew there could be so many stairs in a castle!"

Greedy Greta quickly started the helicopter. "There's no escape, Greedy Greta," said Larryboy.

But what Larryboy didn't know was that the helicopter was equipped with a smelt-flavored pudding squirter.

FWOOOSH!

A stream of yucky brown pudding knocked Larryboy backward. Greedy Greta began to take off. "Pudding won't save you this time!" said Larryboy as he hopped up and shot his plunger ears at the helicopter. But the plungers were covered with pudding and wouldn't stick. "Whadda you know," he said. "Maybe pudding *will* save you after all."

"You'll never catch me now!" said Greedy Greta.

Larryboy had to think fast. His plungers were useless. All at once he realized that he had a secret weapon to use against Greedy Greta: her own greediness!

"Greedy Greta," he shouted. "You left something behind. You might want it!"

"Something I might want?" she greedily shouting over the noise of the helicopter. "What is it? What could it be?"

Larryboy pulled the toy sheep from behind his back.

"My toy sheep. He's really cute!"

Greedy Greta grabbed a pair of binoculars and looked at the sheep. It gave a cute little **"BAAAA."**

"That toy sheep! I want it! I want that toy sheep," she shouted.

A glass tube extended down and sucked the sheep up into the helicopter.

"What a fabulous little sheep! How did I ever live without it? I love it! But...I'll need more toy sheep! One is not enough. I will need more! More sheep, I say!"

But then something happened. The helicopter began to tilt and rock. The addition of the toy sheep had made the helicopter too heavy to fly. Within moments the helicopter fell back down with a thud.

"Come on, you silly helicopter!" said Greedy Greta. But she was too greedy to lighten the load even one little bit, so the helicopter simply couldn't fly.

Larryboy hopped closer and shot a plunger ear at Greedy Greta, wrapping the plunger cord around and around her. "Sorry, Greedy Greta," said Larryboy, "but you're grounded."

CHAPTER 18

HOW ABOUT SOME MORE CLOG DANCING?

A few days later, with Greedy Greta the Greedy Zucchini safely in jail, Larryboy stood on stage at the Bumblyburg Music Hall. The world's greatest yodelers in their *Tribute to Larryboy* concert were serenading him and the toy sheep.

Everyone applauded as the yodelers finished their yodeling. Even Bob.

Einger hopped over and stood beside Larryboy. "Larryboy, we want to thank you!" he said. "Without you, the world would be deprived of quality yodeling entertainment. Not only that, but all of us yodelers would still be stuck inside glass tubes, fearing that smelt-flavored pudding could be dropped onto our heads at any second. Bumblyburg should be proud to have such a hero!"

"I...AM...THAT...HERO!" said Larryboy.

"BAAAA," said the toy sheep.

The crowd applauded again. When the applause died down, Larryboy continued. "Thanks, everyone! I'm honored to serve and guard Bumblyburg against all crazy, dastardly foes! I learned something when fighting Greedy Greta, the Greedy Zucchini. You shouldn't base your happiness on material things. You'll just end up wanting more and more, and that will leave you so unhappy."

Vicki Cucumber sighed, "That Larryboy is just *so* cute!"

"Furthermore, I've decided to donate most of my collection of Hula Friends to kids who may not have their own. I realize now that I really don't need as many as I thought I did."

Backstage, Archie smiled. Larryboy truly had learned something.

"Now, since we're all here in the music hall, I wondered if everyone would like to hear me perform the polka song that defeated Greedy Greta? Hit it, Einger!"

Einger and the other yodelers surrounded Larryboy and began to pull him offstage. "Um, maybe not, Larryboy. I mean, last time you sang that song, you ended up short circuiting a whole army of toys!"

"OK. Well, how about some more clog dancing? Come on! I have worked up a brand-new number. You'll love it!"

"BAAAA," said the toy sheep.

THE END

Book 1:
LarryBoy and the Emperor of Envy
IBSN 978-0-310-70467-6

Book 2:
LarryBoy and the Awful
Ear Wacks Attacks
ISBN 978-0-310-70468-3

Book 3:
LarryBoy and the Sinister Snow Day
ISBN 978-0-310-70561-1

Book 4:
LarryBoy and the Yodelnapper
ISBN 978-0-310-70562-8

Book 5:
LarryBoy in the Good, the Bad,
and the Eggly
ISBN 978-0-310-70650-2

Book 6:
LarryBoy in the Attack
of Outback Jack
ISBN 978-0-310-70649-6

Available now at your local bookstore!

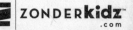